LEVEL
2

MINECRAFT

ESCAPE FROM
THE NETHER

First published in the United States by Random House Children's Books
and in Canada by Penguin Random House Canada Limited.

First published in Great Britain in 2022 by Farshore
An imprint of HarperCollins*Publishers*
1 London Bridge Street, London SE1 9GF
www.farshore.co.uk

HarperCollins*Publishers*
1st Floor, Watermarque Building, Ringsend Road
Dublin 4, Ireland

Written by Nick Eliopulos
Illustrated by Alan Batson

MOJANG
STUDIOS

ISBN 978 0 7555 0046 8
Printed in UK by Martins the Printers
1

Stay safe online. Farshore is not responsible for content hosted by third parties.
Farshore takes its responsibility to the planet and its inhabitants very seriously.
We aim to use papers from well-managed forests run by responsible suppliers.

MIX
Paper from
responsible sources
FSC™ C007454

FSC
www.fsc.org

This book is produced from independently certified FSC™ paper
to ensure responsible forest management.

For more information visit: www.harpercollins.co.uk/green

Reading Together

Before you start reading, it helps to talk about what
you think might happen in the story.

Have you seen these characters before?
What will happen to them?
Does the title help you?
Are there any clues on the cover?

Sound out unfamiliar words and look for clues in the pictures.
Sometimes the words before and after an unknown word can
help you work out what a difficult word means.

After you've finished the story, go back to any words that
you found tricky and talk about what they mean.
This helps you to remember them!

Activities for After Reading

Can you spot these challenging words in this story?

loyal   portal   obsidian   gasped   fungi

inventory   fortress   lava   chirping

What does each word mean? How do you know?
Does the sentence help? Can you put the word into another
sentence? Talk about what you think the next adventure for
Emmy, Birch and Byte will be.

Question Time!

Why did Birch and Emmy go into the forest? Why did
they enter the portal? Did they find what they were looking for?

Advanced Questions

How do we know that the piglins like gold?
Can you find three clues in the story that tell you?

Emmy and Birch
were ready for adventure!
Emmy had a brand new helmet
and matching boots made of
yellow gold. Birch had a brand new
sword made of iron.

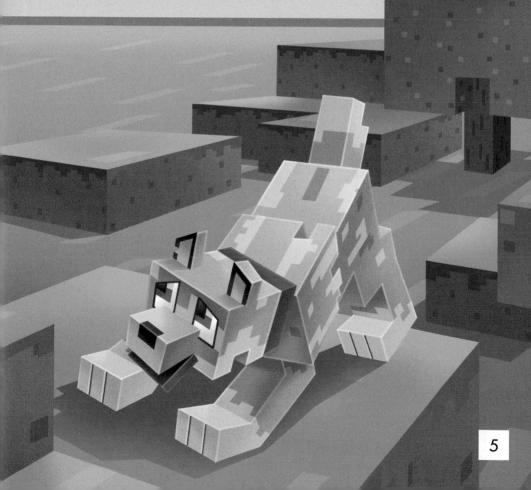

Byte, their loyal wolf,
just wanted to play.
"We can play fetch,"
said Emmy.
"Ready, boy?"
asked Birch.

"FETCH!"

Byte ran after the stick.
But he did not return.
"Where did he go?"
asked Birch.
They both called him.

They did not find Byte,
but they saw something
strange. Beneath the trees,
they found a rectangle
of blocks made of black
obsidian. The air glowed
purple inside it.

"It's a portal
to the Nether,"
said Emmy.
She put her hand
into the purple light.
Her hand disappeared!

"Do you think Byte
went through the portal?"
asked Birch.
"There is only one way
to find out," said Emmy.
"Come on!"

The two friends
leaped into the portal.
At first, Birch thought
they were still in the forest.

Then he saw that
the trees were
blue-green.
So was the grass.

13

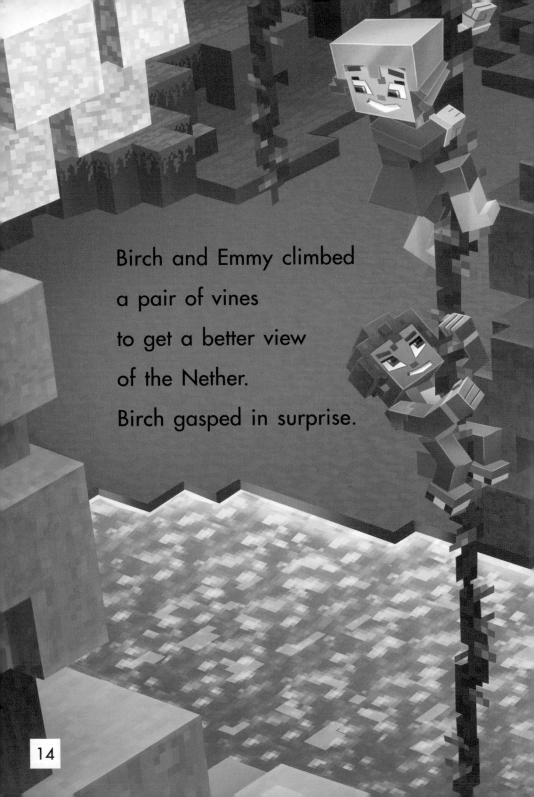

Birch and Emmy climbed
a pair of vines
to get a better view
of the Nether.
Birch gasped in surprise.

He saw a grey desert.

He saw a red woodland.

And he saw an ocean of lava.

Birch had never seen any place
like this in Minecraft.
"Even the mushrooms are strange!"
Emmy told him with a laugh.
She put two blue-green fungi
in her inventory.

Setting out to find Byte,
they started walking.
The strange blue-green forest
became a strange red forest.

Birch raised his hand.

They were being watched.

Birch's warning was too late.

Strange mobs surrounded them.

"Piglins!" cried Emmy.

The piglins attacked Birch!
But they left Emmy alone.
They liked her gold helmet
and gold boots.

Emmy had an idea!
She took off her gold helmet
and put it on Birch's head.
The piglins stopped
fighting Birch.

The mobs oinked
with happiness.
Emmy and Birch
followed them
to a huge fortress.

In the fortress, they found a
treasure room filled with gold.
Birch opened a chest.
The piglins drew their swords
and made angry noises!

Emmy and Birch escaped
the mobs by smashing a
big hole in the wall. On the
other side was a desert.

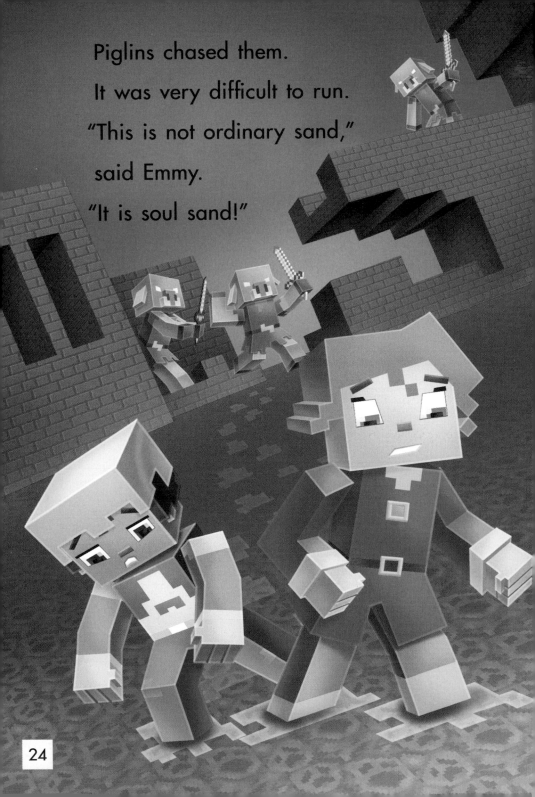

Piglins chased them.
It was very difficult to run.
"This is not ordinary sand,"
said Emmy.
"It is soul sand!"

Skeletons also started
firing arrows at them!
Emmy and Birch ran faster.
They could see a portal
on the other side of
a river of lava!

"We're trapped," said Birch.
Emmy pointed at two striders
with red skin and stringy hair.
"We can't cross the lava,"
said Emmy, "but striders can!"

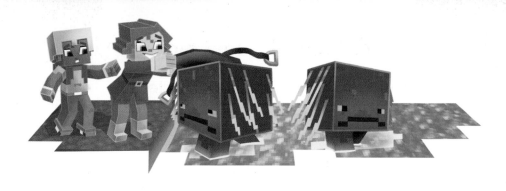

Emmy saddled the striders.
She and Birch climbed onto
the passive mobs, but the
striders stood there, chirping.

Emmy offered them carrots.
They just kept chirping.
Birch had an idea.
Carrots did not grow
in the Nether. Maybe
striders did not eat them.

"Quick! Offer them the blue-green fungi," Birch shouted, as a floating ghast joined the skeletons and piglins.

When the striders saw
the fungi, they started
running! Emmy and
Birch raced toward
the portal.

On the other side of the portal,

they could see Byte.

He was waiting for them.

He had his stick in his mouth.

They were going to make it!

Safe in the Overworld,
Emmy threw the stick.
Byte fetched it, and
then Birch threw it.
Playing with Byte
was a great end
to a great adventure!

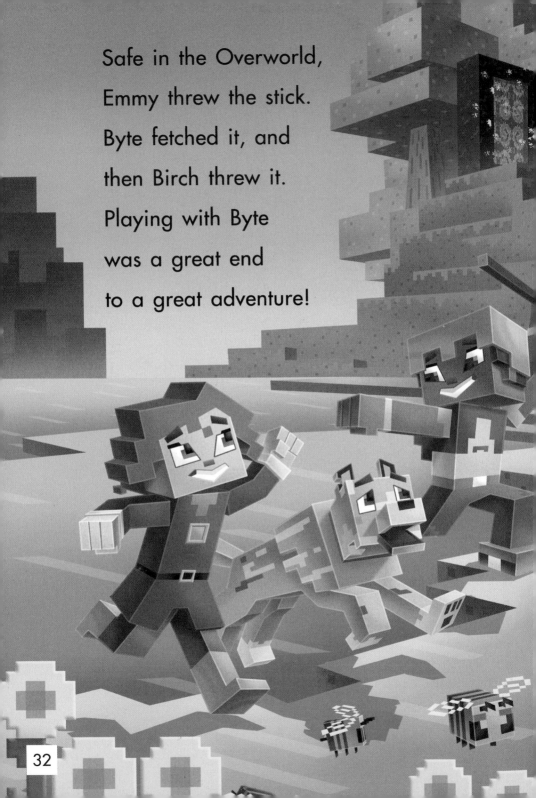